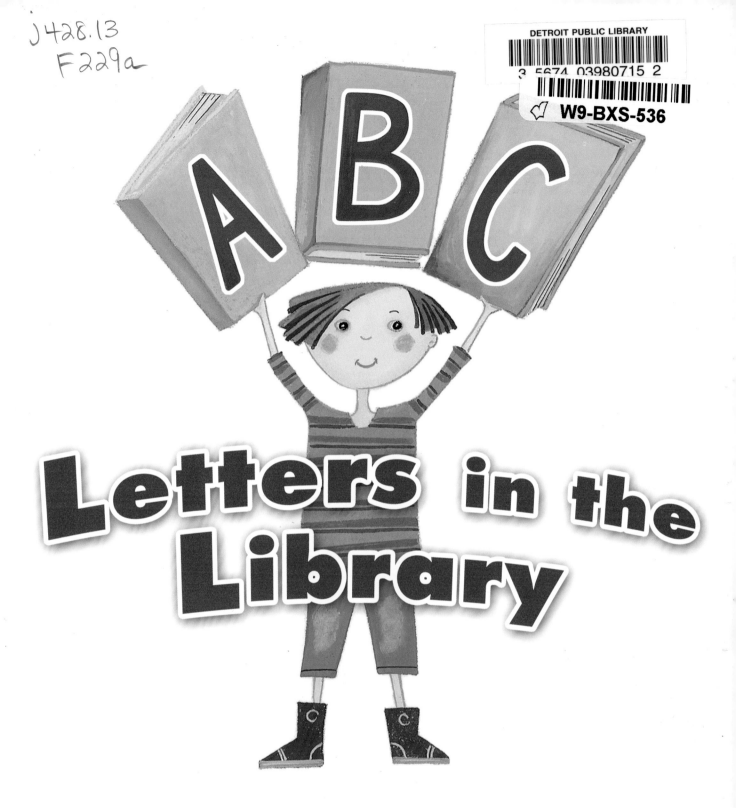

A B C Letters in the Library

written by
Bonnie Farmer

illustrated by
Chum McLeod

Lobster Press ™

Published in 2005 by:
Lobster Press™
1620 Sherbrooke Street West, Suites C & D
Montréal, Québec   H3H 1C9
Tel. (514) 904-1100 • Fax (514) 904-1101
www.lobsterpress.com

Publisher: Alison Fripp
Editors: Alison Fripp & Karen Li
Graphic Design & Production: Tammy Desnoyers

We acknowledge the financial support of the Government
of Canada through the Book Publishing Industry
Development Program (BPIDP) for our publishing activities.

We acknowledge the support of
the Canada Council for the Arts
for our publishing program.

Library and Archives Canada Cataloguing in Publication

Farmer, Bonnie, 1959-
        ABC letters in the library / Bonnie Farmer ; illustrated by
Chum McLeod.

ISBN 1-894222-87-3 (bound).-ISBN 1-897073-19-4 (pbk.)

        1. Libraries--Juvenile literature. 2. Alphabet books. 3. English
language--Alphabet--Juvenile literature. I. McLeod, Chum II. Title.

Z665.5.F37 2004   j027   C2004-901420-X

Printed and bound in Canada.

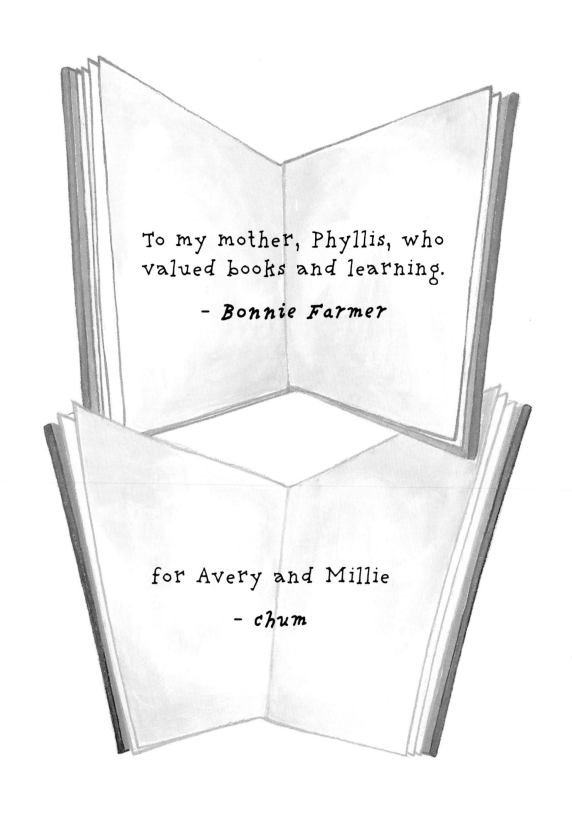

To my mother, Phyllis, who valued books and learning.

– *Bonnie Farmer*

for Avery and Millie

– *chum*

Aisles of authors are arranged alphabetically.

Beautiful books dazzle browsing bookworms.

Humming computers collect countless call numbers.

Dense dictionaries unravel difficult terms.

Encyclopedias teach the most earnest of learners.

Ff

Fun-filled ghost stories frighten and shock.

Spinning globes
gather great dreams
of travel.

The librarian's soft *shhh* soon **h**ushes all talk.

Hh

Information flows freely in and out of the Internet.

A smooth glossy jacket is a book's best protection.

Jj

Kk

Searching for knowledge keeps kids' minds wide open.

A librarian's friendship leaves lasting impressions.

Members view maps through magnifying glasses,

Mm

while nappers nod off behind inky newspapers.

Nn

Overdue
books keep
all **o**thers
waiting.

Bright **p**ages burst with eye-**p**leasing **p**ictures.

Inquisitive ones quietly ask lots of questions.

Qq

A reader floats off on
a soft Persian rug.

Rr

Ss

Story time spreads smiles on small students' faces.

Tt

Teachers *tsk* at loud teens,
who grin and then shrug.

Used books are
donated by
bighearted readers,

Uu

Then put into place by **V**aluable **V**olunteers.

Writers weave wonderful words with their pencils.

the wizard waved his magic wand.

Young artists' eXhibits receive praise and cheers.

Youngsters shuffle home bearing books that they love,

And pages become pillows as stars shine above.
Zzzzzz.